Dear Parent:

Your child's love of reading starts here!

Every child learns to read in a different way and at his or her own speed. Some go back and forth between reading levels and read favorite books again and again. Others read through each level in order. You can help your young reader improve and become more confident by encouraging his or her own interests and abilities. From books your child reads with you to the first books he or she reads alone, there are I Can Read Books for every stage of reading:

SHARED READING
Basic language, word repetition, and whimsical illustrations, ideal for sharing with your emergent reader

BEGINNING READING
Short sentences, familiar words, and simple concepts for children eager to read on their own

READING WITH HELP
Engaging stories, longer sentences, and language play for developing readers

READING ALONE
Complex plots, challenging vocabulary, and high-interest topics for the independent reader

I Can Read Books have introduced children to the joy of reading since 1957. Featuring award-winning authors and illustrators and a fabulous cast of beloved characters, I Can Read Books set the standard for beginning readers.

A lifetime of discovery begins with the magical words "I Can Read!"

Visit www.icanread.com for information
on enriching your child's reading experience.

Pinkalicious
Treasuretastic

For Zoe
—V.K.

The author gratefully acknowledges
the artistic and editorial contributions of
Daniel Griffo and Jacqueline Resnick.

I Can Read® and I Can Read Book® are trademarks of HarperCollins Publishers.

Pinkalicious: Treasuretastic
Copyright © 2021 by VBK, Co.

PINKALICIOUS and all related logos and characters are trademarks of Victoria Kann. Used with permission.

Based on the HarperCollins book *Pinkalicious* written by
Victoria Kann and Elizabeth Kann, illustrated by Victoria Kann
All rights reserved. Printed in the United States of America.
No part of this book may be used or reproduced in any manner whatsoever without
written permission except in the case of brief quotations embodied in critical articles and reviews.
For information address HarperCollins Children's Books, a division of HarperCollins Publishers,
195 Broadway, New York, NY 10007.
www.icanread.com

ISBN 978-0-06-300379-8 (trade bdg.)—ISBN 978-0-06-300378-1 (pbk.)

22 23 24 25 LSCC 10 9 8 7 6 5 4 3 2
❖
First Edition

BEGINNING 1 READING

I Can Read!

Pinkalicious
Treasuretastic

by Victoria Kann

HARPER

An Imprint of HarperCollinsPublishers

"I'm ready to hike!"

I said to my little brother, Peter.

I twirled to show off

my new pinkatastic pants.

"Look at all my pockets," I said.
"They're perfect for collecting
treasures!"
"Can I collect treasures, too?"
Peter asked.

"Yes!" I said.

"Let's play Treasure Hunters!
Whoever finds the best
treasure wins."

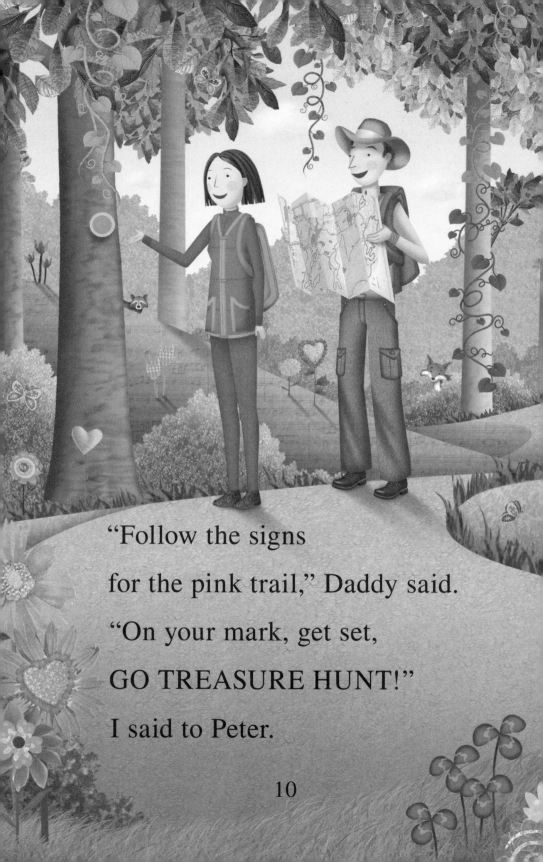

"Follow the signs
for the pink trail," Daddy said.
"On your mark, get set,
GO TREASURE HUNT!"
I said to Peter.

I saw pinkapretty berries.

"I spot treasure!" I said.

"Look what I found!" Peter said
at the same time.

I gasped when I saw what Peter had.

"A four-leaf clover?" I said.

"How did you find that?"

"I guess I'm lucky," Peter said.

I put my berries in

one of my pockets.

They didn't seem
so exciting anymore.
"I'm going to find something
even better," I said.
"It will be treasuretastic!"

I collected a yellow buttercup.

I found a teeny tiny pinecone.

I filled my pockets

with handfuls of seeds,

perfect acorns,

leaves, and flowers

in every color.

My treasures were pretty,
but they still weren't as good
as Peter's four-leaf clover.

"I guess I'm not a great treasure hunter," I said.

We reached a clearing
at the top of the hill.
"You can see all of Pinkville
from here," Daddy said.

17

"There's our house!" Mommy said.

"I see Mr. Swizzle's

ice cream shop," Daddy added.

"Everything is so tiny," Peter said.

"Come look, Pinkalicious!"

"Not now," I said to Peter.

"I'm too busy searching

for treasure!"

A pink bird landed on the shrub.
"Do you know where
I can find a pinkatastic,
pinkaperfect treasure?"
I asked the bird.

"Tweet, tweet!" the birdy chirped.
Suddenly I spotted something
next to it!

"Guess what, Peter," I said.
"I found the most pinkamazing
treasure in the forest!"
I held out a perfectly pink,
heart-shaped leaf.

"I found a heart, too!" Peter said.

He showed me a pink

heart-shaped rose.

23

I couldn't believe Peter found
a better treasure again!
I stomped off
to collect more treasures.

My pockets were bursting,

but I could not stop.

I heard a pitter-patter.

A cute bunny was following us.

So was the pink bird.

"What are they eating?" Peter asked.

An acorn fell from my pocket.

A squirrel came to nibble at it.

"My pockets are leaking." I gasped.

"The animals are eating

my treasures!"

"I think they like them," Peter said.

More animals came over.

"Oh, deer!" I said

as a deer joined the group.

"Look at all the animals," Peter said.

"I've never seen anything like it,"

said Mommy.

I patted my torn pockets.

"It's all because of my treasures,"

I said proudly.

"Thank you, Pinkalicious,"

Daddy said.

"What a special day!"

"You're welcome," I said.

"But I'm not the only one to thank."

I waved to the woodland animals.

"Thank you!" I called to them.

"I'll treasure this hike forever!"